Ten Things
I LOVE About YOU

DANIEL KIRK

Nancy Paulsen Books 🌀 An Imprint of Penguin Group (USA) Inc.

Look at this—
I am making a list!

Number 1—I love Pig
because he is very pink.
That's nice, Rabbit,
but that's only one thing.
Didn't you say there
were ten?

Oh, that gives me an idea!
Number 2—I love Pig
because he knows how
to keep busy.

Yes, Rabbit, I am busy.
So why don't you go and
think about the other
things you want to write?

Okay, Pig,
I'll be back soon!

Oh, I have another one!
Number 3—I love Pig
because he believes in me.

I do believe in you, Rabbit.
But ten things is a lot.
You don't have to write
that many!

I want to, but I'm a slow writer! Maybe you could write my ideas down for me?

You can do it, Rabbit. You're a good writer!

Oh, perfect.
*Number 4—I love Pig
because he gives good
compliments.*

TEN THINGS I LOVE ABOUT PIG.
1. I love Pig because he is very pink.
2. I love Pig because he knows how to keep busy.
3. I love Pig because he believes in me.
4. I love Pig because he gives good compliments.

Rabbit, I'm really busy now. Could you come back later, and we'll do something fun?

Fantastic!
Number 5—I love Pig because he's full of good ideas.

Rabbit, I'm starting to lose my patience!

Number 6—I love Pig because he's not afraid to show his feelings.

Number 7—I love Pig
because he is polite
and always says please.

Rabbit, *please* go
finish your list.
Later we'll play any
game you want!

Number 8—I love Pig
because he knows how
much I like to play games.
Just two more things and
my list will be done!

Hello, Pig!
I thought and thought,
but I still have only
eight things on my list.

Eight things are plenty,
Rabbit. Thank you.
You can give me
your list now!

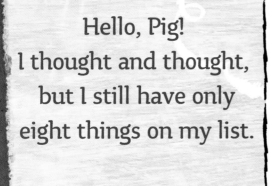

Wait!
Number 9—I love Pig
because he doesn't want
me to work too hard.

Hey, Pig,
what's that
you dropped?

It's just something
I'm making, Rabbit.
it's . . . a list.

It says *Ten Things
I Love About Rabbit!*
Oh, Pig! That's great!
You were making
a list, too!

Yes, Rabbit. Can you believe
we both had the same idea!

That's because we're
such good friends!
I know what Number 10 is—
*I love Pig
because he's my friend.*

You're my friend too,
Rabbit!

TEN THINGS I LOVE ABOUT PiG.

1. I love Pig ~~bek~~ because he is very pink.

2. I love Pig because he knows how to keep busy.

3. I love Pig because he believes in me.

4. I love Pig because he gives good compliments.

5. I love Pig because he's full of good ideas.

6. I love Pig because he's not afraid to show his feelings.

7. I love Pig because he is polite and always says *please*.

8. I love Pig because he knows how much I like to play games.

9. I love Pig because he doesn't want me to work too hard.

10. I love Pig because he's my friend.

Love, Rabbit ☺

TEN

~~Five~~ Things I
Love about Rabbit

1. I love Rabbit because he always drops by.
2. I love Rabbit because he smiles so much.
3. I love Rabbit because he gets so excited about things.
4. I love Rabbit because he leaves when I'm busy.
5. I love Rabbit because he's not afraid to ask for help.
6. I love Rabbit because he always sees the good side.
7. I love Rabbit because he never gives up.
8. I love Rabbit because he's always thinking.
9. I love Rabbit because he's funny.
10. I love Rabbit because he's my friend.

Love, Pig ♥

for Fiona

NANCY PAULSEN BOOKS · A division of Penguin Young Readers Group.
Published by The Penguin Group.
Penguin Group (USA) Inc., 375 Hudson Street, New York, NY 10014, U.S.A.
Penguin Group (Canada), 90 Eglinton Avenue East, Suite 700, Toronto,
Ontario M4P 2Y3, Canada (a division of Pearson Penguin Canada Inc.).
Penguin Books Ltd, 80 Strand, London WC2R 0RL, England.
Penguin Ireland, 25 St. Stephen's Green, Dublin 2, Ireland
(a division of Penguin Books Ltd).
Penguin Group (Australia), 250 Camberwell Road, Camberwell, Victoria 3124,
Australia (a division of Pearson Australia Group Pty Ltd).
Penguin Books India Pvt Ltd, 11 Community Centre,
Panchsheel Park, New Delhi - 110 017, India.
Penguin Group (NZ), 67 Apollo Drive, Rosedale, Auckland 0632,
New Zealand (a division of Pearson New Zealand Ltd).
Penguin Books (South Africa) (Pty) Ltd, 24 Sturdee Avenue,
Rosebank, Johannesburg 2196, South Africa.
Penguin Books Ltd, Registered Offices: 80 Strand, London WC2R 0RL, England.

Design by Annie Ericsson.
Text set in Century Schoolbook Std and Tyke ITC Std. Hand lettering by Annie Ericsson.
The illustrations in this book were made by scanning ink-on-paper drawings and painted
plywood panels into the computer and adding textures and colors in Photoshop.
Library of Congress Cataloging-in-Publication Data
Kirk, Daniel. Ten things I love about you / Daniel Kirk. p. cm.
Summary: Rabbit makes a list of the things he loves about Pig,
but needs Pig's help deciding what to write.
[1. Friendship—Fiction. 2. Pigs—Fiction. 3. Rabbits—Fiction.] I. Title.
PZ7.K6339Ten 2013 [E]—dc23 2012011081
ISBN 978-0-399-25288-4
1 3 5 7 9 10 8 6 4 2

ALWAYS LEARNING   PEARSON